Infinity

Pablo Bernasconi

Penny Candy Books

Oklahoma City & Greensboro

 This book is printed on paper certified to the environmental and social standards of the Forest Stewardship Council™ (FSC®).

Photo of Pablo Bernasconi: Alejandra Bartoliche

Design adaptation for English edition: Shanna Compton

∞ You'll notice numbers, symbols, and equations on the subsequent pages. Some are mathematical, others scientific; some are personal, others mystical or mythical. But all of them capture and represent a take on the concept of infinity.

Small press. Big conversations.

www.pennycandybooks.com

Library of Congress Cataloging-in-Publication Data

Names: Bernasconi, Pablo, 1973- author, illustrator.

Title: Infinity / Pablo Bernasconi.

Other titles: Infinito. English

Description: Oklahoma City & Greensboro : Penny Candy Books, 2021. | Audience: Ages 9 and up | Audience: Grades 4-6

Identifiers: LCCN 2020017933 | ISBN 9781734225921 (hardcover) | ISBN 9781736031940 (ebook)

Subjects: LCSH: Infinity--Juvenile literature.

Classification: LCC BD411 .B42613 2021 | DDC 111/.6--dc23

LC record available at https://lccn.loc.gov/2020017933

25 24 23 22 21   1 2 3 4 5

For Nina and Franco, for Tania,

my infinite present

I could be bounded
in a nutshell,
and count myself
a King
of infinite space...

William Shakespeare

$$x_{t+1} = kx_t(1-x_t)$$

It's

that nightmare

where I'm inside the snow of a television screen,

and I have to sweep it up

with a toothpick.

It's

a grain of sand

lost in a desert somewhere in the world

that contains

an engraved map

for finding yourself.

E = hv

It's

the exact moment between awake and asleep.

Those who manage to remain there

freeze this moment forever.

$$f(x) = ae - \frac{(x-b)^2}{2c^2}$$

It's

a very thin line

that thinks it must dance

en pointe

even when it's alone.

$G_{\mu\nu} = 8\pi G T_{\mu\nu}$

It's

an ant that lost its place in line

and wanders confidently

between an elephant's legs.

$e^{i\pi} + 1 = 0$

It's

reading only the last line of a book

and imagining the rest of it.

6.022×10^{23}

It's

the inside

of a big lady's black skirt

as seen by a germ.

$\Delta S \geq 0$

It's

a castaway who believes

that if she emptied all the water from the sea

with a cup

she could simply walk home.

It's

a musical box

full of silence.

It's

the eye of an artist

just before

he starts drawing.

$i\hbar\gamma^{\mu}\partial_{\mu}\psi - mc\psi = 0$

It's

a carpenter

waiting for the love of his life

in the wrong life.

It's

a

dreaming

angel.

It's

an idea that doesn't want to,

doesn't let itself,

refuses to be caged

in one word.

K = 100

It's

a giant white tapestry

that hides the first gray hair

of a black sheep.

$\lambda = h/p$

It's

a glass of water,

a burning building,

and a thirsty

fireman.

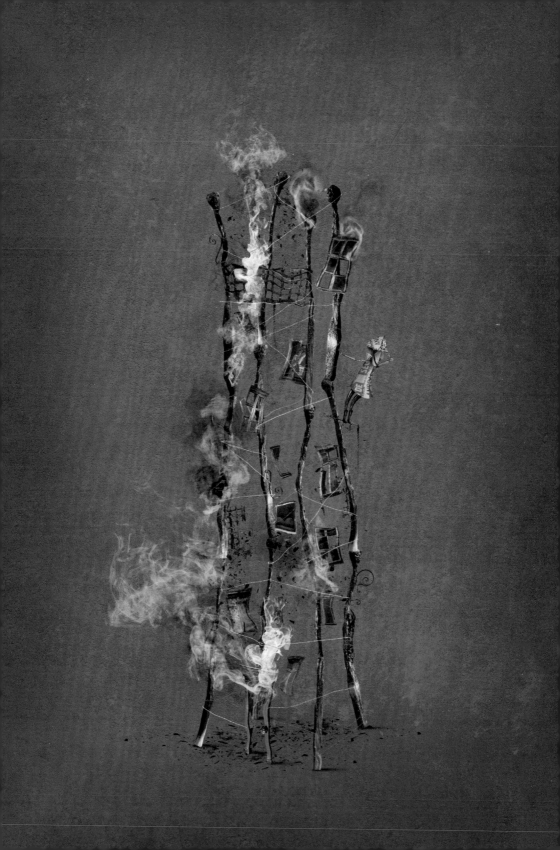

Å

It's

two particles of dust

playing hide-and-go-seek

on different planets.

$\varepsilon = \omega^{\varepsilon}$

It's

a krill who savors

the palate of a whale

and believes it is a banquet.

It's

the pencil lead—

swallowed by the sharpener—

that would have written

the solution to everything.

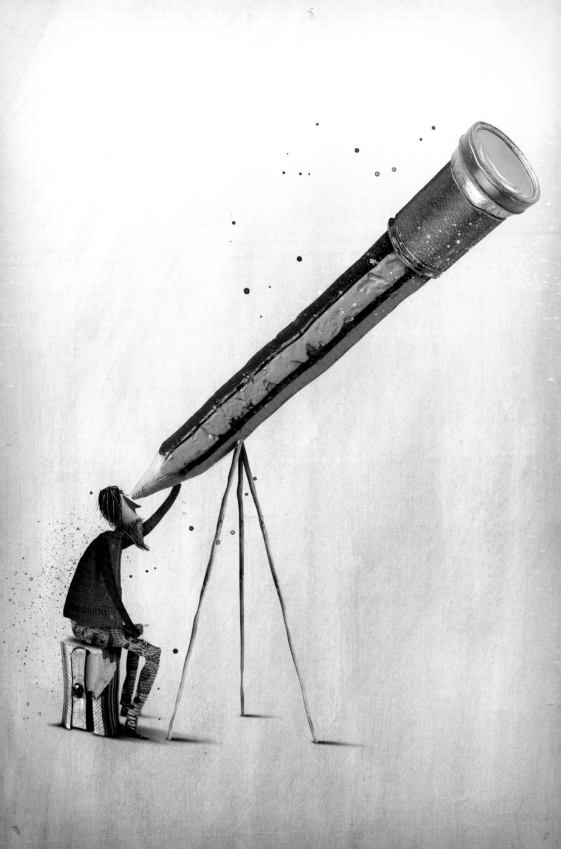

It's

abandoning a book

just before the part

that would have changed our lives.

$$i\hbar\frac{d}{dt}|\Psi(t)\rangle = \hat{H}|\Psi(t)\rangle$$

It's

a jar full of stories and white ink

spilled

on the snow.

$E = mc^2$

It's

the instruction manual

to the machine

that operates

the sun and stars.

$n_i + 1 = 1$

It's

the formula for happiness

hidden in a cow's hide.

But on the inside.

$\Phi = 1.6180339887$

It's
a golden sunrise
and a painter with a huge tube
of gray oil paint.

$v = H_0 d$

It's

the starriest of nights,

and no one can see anything

because it's cloudy.

It's

a story

that survived my childhood,

and I only understand it now that I am grown-up.

Is it too late?

3.141592653589793238

It's
a happy ending
that repeats itself
over and over
over and over
over and over
over and over
over and over
over and over
over and over
over and over
over and over

Pablo Bernasconi was born in Buenos Aires, Argentina on August 6, 1973. He is a graphic designer who graduated from the University of Buenos Aires, where he was also a professor of Design and Head of Practical Assignments for five years. He began his career as an illustrator in *Clarín* newspaper in 1998, creating the cover page artwork for more than 350 supplement editions. He also used to publish a critical review in *La Nación* every Sunday. Some of his illustrations have been published in newspapers and magazines all around the world, including the *New York Times*, *Wall Street Journal*, *Saturday Evening Post*, *Telegraph*, and the *Times of England*. Besides his media work, Pablo is a continuous collaborator with the human rights organization Grandmothers of the Plaza de Mayo for their design and graphic projects. He is the award-winning author and illustrator of sixteen books, and he has illustrated another twenty books by other authors.

Curious about the numbers, symbols, and equations on these pages? Some are mathematical, others scientific; some are personal, others mystical and mythical.

Check out **pennycandybooks.com/infinity** to learn more!